Merry Christmas
James + Benji
♡

Mary Jinnie

# SIDEWALK PROPHETS
# the Luckiest Star

**written by**
David Frey & Ben McDonald
with Elizabeth Cardella

**illustrated by**
David Leonard

# Dedicated to
# William & Theodore

Copyright © 2022 by Dave Frey and Ben McDonald

All rights reserved. No part of this publication may be reproduced or transmitted in any form or by any means, electronic or mechanical, including photocopying, recording, or by other electronic or mechanical methods, without the prior written permission of the publisher. For permission requests, email bookinquiries@sidewalkprophets.com.

Published by Sidewalk Prophets
188 Front Street, Suite 116-44
Franklin, TN 37064
www.sidewalkprophets.com

ISBN 79-8-9868693-0-8

Printed in the United States of America First Edition, 2022

Ordering Information
For wholesale orders by U.S. trade bookstores, corporations, associations and others, contact bookinquiries@sidewalkprophets.com

Design by hybridstudios.com
Illustration by davidleonard.com

# Dear Children
of the older kind (the ones we call adults),

**Every once upon a time** we are reminded about things that are true, even if they are embedded inside a song, story, parable, line in a movie, a whisper. When we are reminded, and we remember, a truth, a hope, a mystery, a whisper…something deep is rebuilt. The opposite of remember is not to forget, it is to dismember.

**This is a beautiful little book** about remembering. I dare you to read it and not have something resonate in the deep places, the stirring of remembering. When you read it to the children in your life they will delight, which is a way of remembering. *Remembering that they each matter and that they each are an intricately crafted and unique expression of love in the world.* Their presence alone changes the cosmos, like Hemmy, the star in this story, like…you!

**So**, listen…and remember, and **sing** and **dance** and **whisper**… and remember. And cry…and remember.

Paul Young
Author, *The Shack*

Throughout the years, the story of Christmas has been told many times and in many ways.

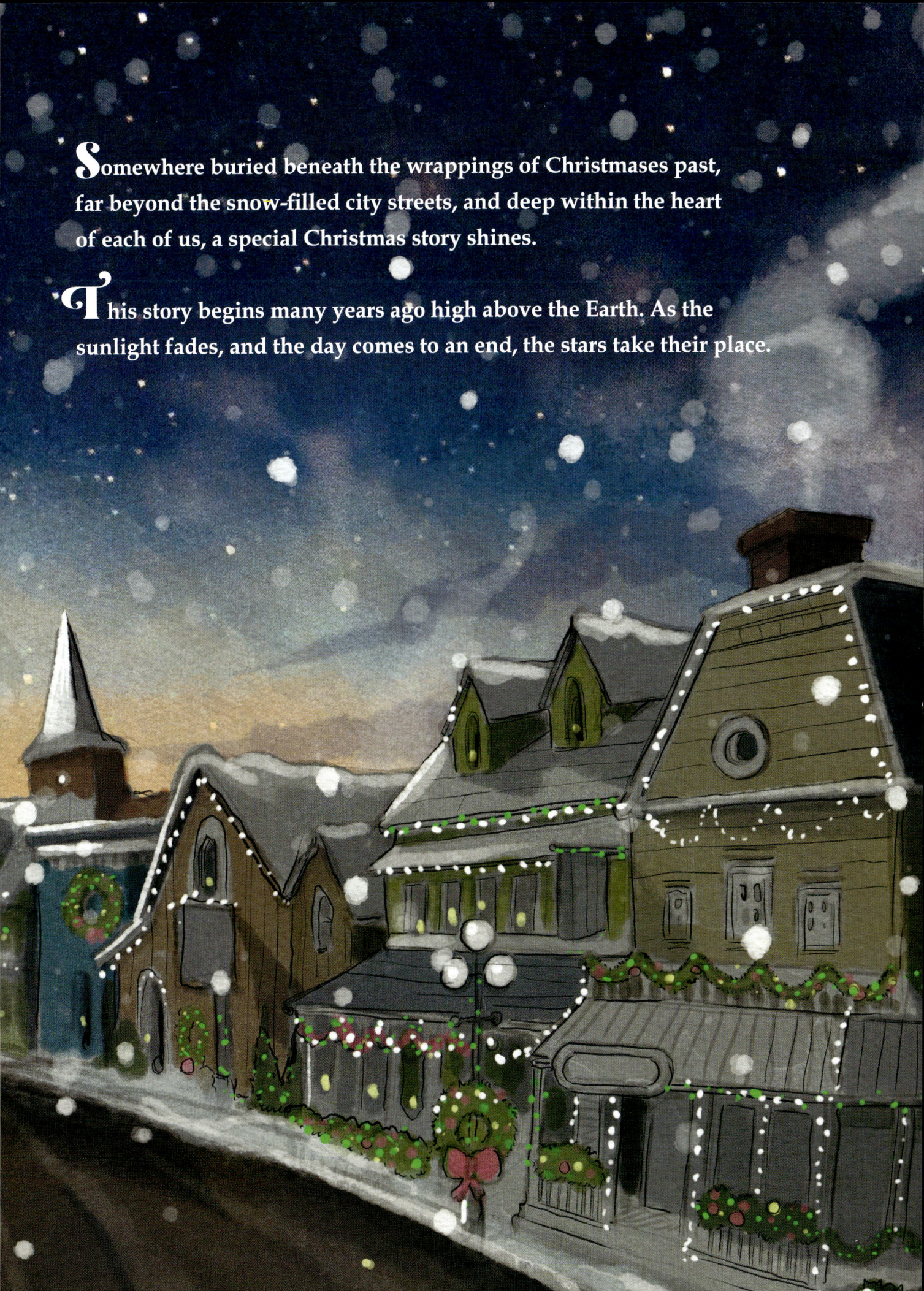

**S**omewhere buried beneath the wrappings of Christmases past, far beyond the snow-filled city streets, and deep within the heart of each of us, a special Christmas story shines.

**T**his story begins many years ago high above the Earth. As the sunlight fades, and the day comes to an end, the stars take their place.

Some stars are so big, they can be seen from galaxies far away. Some form groups and create constellations, painting pictures across the universe. Some stars move, and some stay put. Some shine bright, and some like to run, leaving trails of light behind them. This story is about an altogether uninteresting star. He wasn't the biggest star in the sky. He wasn't the brightest either. He was a curious and lively star named Hemmy.

**H**emmy loved to explore everything around him. He was always searching, always wondering. He could see that the sun's job was to light up the day, and that the moon's glow helped give shape to the night. Seeing that everyone had a purpose, he wondered,
  Why was he made? Where was his place?
     Where did he fit in?

**O**ne thing he knew for sure was that he loved to sing.
He would sing and sing, then sing some more.
Even when the other stars were far too busy,
Hemmy would sing with all his heart.

He would sing to his best friend, the moon, every night. They would laugh and dance together. They would stay up late and watch the world, hoping to see something special. The other stars would all look down. They would see Hemmy singing too loud and laughing too much.

One day, the other stars all got together. They decided enough was enough. A star's job was important, not something to sing about. They sent the brightest star in the universe, a royal star named Sir, to talk to Hemmy and put an end to all the noise and mischief.

Sir said to the little star, "Why don't you act more like us? The Maker made each of us for a purpose. We form our constellations and stand together. We take shape and shine bright. We are always in our place. What a silly star you are."

Hemmy was heartbroken, though he didn't want to show it. That night, his song turned to tears and his laughter to sadness. The little star decided, then and there, to change his ways. No more singing. No more laughing. No more dancing. If he was ever going to be important, he would have to be more like the others.

He was going to grow up and take shape.
Hemmy went and stood amongst the constellations.
He found a perfect spot at the end of the Big Dipper.
"Surely here I can fit in," thought Hemmy.

The moon leaned in to watch his friend.
But just then, a cosmic wind began to bluster.
Stardust stirred and blew right past the moon's nose.

The moon made a very funny face and sneezed. It started as a giggle, but Hemmy couldn't keep his laughter inside. His laugh was so loud it shook all the stars in the Big Dipper.

"Hemmy, your laughter is making us lose our place!" said the other stars. "We have to stick together. You don't know our routine. Go away and don't come back!"

With his heart full of frowns, Hemmy left to find someplace else to belong.

**N**ext, Hemmy went to see the North Star, known around the galaxy as Polly. In all her years of service, Polly had never moved, not even once. She was a legend among the stars. Hemmy slowly approached Polly. He took a deep breath and asked, "Would it be all right if I glowed beside you tonight? You could teach me how to stand at attention and shine bright. I would like to be more like you."

"**I**f you think you have what it takes, you can try," Polly replied.

That night, Hemmy stood as still as he could. It was hard, really hard. Hemmy had never stood so still in his life. As he stood, his mind started to wander and play.

**T**hen, his heart started to create a song. It was a cheerful song with a catchy rhythm and an out-of-this-world beat. It started as a wiggle, but with the song moving in his mind, heart, and feet, Hemmy had to dance. He danced a wild, thankful dance.

**W**hen his dance finally finished, Polly was annoyed. "I gave you a chance," she said. "I was made to guide the world below. I never waiver and always shine. You could never be like me. Now, please leave and don't come back. I have a long night of standing perfectly still ahead of me."

At that moment, Hemmy's song was gone.
And the tiny light he carried in his heart refused to shine.
He would never find his place. He would never fit in.
That night the moon went dark, too sad to glow for his friend.

In the middle of the darkness, suddenly, something startling happened. The night flooded with light brighter than the sky had ever known. Full of color and joy, the Maker appeared!

In all His power and glory, He saw Hemmy. With a tender look, He asked, "My dear, dear little star, why are you so sad? What has made such a playful one like you cease to smile?" Hemmy was afraid to tell the truth. But he found a tiny bit of courage, faced the Maker, and cried,

"I am sorry, Maker. I'm a disappointment. I'm too silly to be of any use. I want so much to be something special. I want to sing and laugh and dance. But most of all, I just want to fit in."

The Maker's face grew sorrowful as He replied, "Why would you want to just fit in? Don't you know I made you for a reason? You are more special than you could ever dream. I made you to sing and laugh and dance. I made you to reflect the love I have for you, no matter what others may believe.

I have the most important job of all saved for a star just like you. I made you to sing from your heart, a song of peace, a song of hope, a song of love. Your song will bring joy throughout the universe!"

The little star was in awe. He never knew the Maker had a plan just for him. What a lucky star he was, the luckiest star of all. In that moment, his heart burst with happiness.

The moon had overheard every word the Maker told Hemmy, and in blissful celebration for his friend, he grew full and bright in the sky. They sang and laughed and danced together again.

That very night, far below the heavens, in an unexpected place, the Maker's son was born! Hemmy looked down and saw the baby placed inside a humble manger, and his joy overflowed. He couldn't help himself. He began to shine brighter than ever and sing a new song for the newborn King. Just then, wise men looked up in awe, hearing Hemmy's song in their hearts. They followed his song all the way to a town called Bethlehem. And there, they met the Maker's son,

# Jesus!

Every star in the galaxy heard Hemmy's song. They saw him shine and were amazed. Sir felt his heart stir and began to sing along. All the stars in the Big Dipper started to laugh and shake the sky. And for the first time in a very long time, Polly began to dance. Each and every star had a song, a laugh, and a dance in their heart to celebrate the Maker's son. Hemmy was the brightest of them all.

The whole earth saw Hemmy, the Star of Bethlehem, shining in the night sky. They stared in wide-eyed wonder. They felt the joy of Hope being born. That night, the world was changed forever.

**I**f you listen closely this Christmas, you can still hear the Star of Bethlehem's song, a melody for the ages. And if you look up at the night sky, you might just spot Hemmy, the Luckiest Star, still proudly shining, filling hearts with a thrill of hope, and reflecting the Maker's love for you.

*"Where is the one who has been born king of the Jews? We saw his star when it rose and have come to worship him."* — Matthew 2:2